Old Possum's Book of Practical
CATS

CATS the movie, directed by Academy Award winner, Tom Hooper, is based on Andrew Lloyd Webber's legendary musical, CATS, which, in turn, is based on T. S. Eliot's poetry collection, *Old Possum's Book of Practical Cats*.

T. S. Eliot's playful cat poems have delighted readers and cat lovers around the world ever since they were first published in 1939. They were inspired by letters to his godchildren – for a four-year-old Tom Faber, Eliot wrote a splendid:

Invitation to all pollicle dogs & jellicle cats to come to the birthday of Thomas Faber.

Young Tom invented the words 'pollicle' (for 'poor little' dogs) and 'jellicle' (meaning 'dear little' cats) via mispronunciation and Eliot immortalized them in his whimsical verse, as always using his nom de plume, 'Old Possum'.

This edition includes, for the first time, the poem 'Rhapsody on a Windy Night' which inspired the song 'Memory' in the musical.

FABER AND FABER
has published children's
books since 1929.
Some of our very first
publications included *Old
Possum's Book of Practical
Cats* by T. S. Eliot starring
the now world-famous
Macavity, and *The Iron
Man* by Ted Hughes. Our
catalogue at the time said
that 'it is by reading such
books that children learn
the difference between
the shoddy and the
genuine'. We still believe
in the power of reading
to transform children's
lives.

✈ FABER CLASSICS ✈

○ ○ **T. S. ELIOT** ○ ○

Old Possum's Book of Practical CATS

Illustrated by Rebecca Ashdown

90 YEARS OF EXCELLENCE
FABER & FABER

First published in 1939
by Faber and Faber Limited
Bloomsbury House, 74–77 Great Russell Street, London WC1B 3DA

This edition first published in 2019

Design by Faber & Faber

Printed by CPI Group (UK) Ltd, Croydon CR4 0YY

A CIP record for this book is available from the British Library

ISBN 978–0–571–35983–7

2 4 6 8 10 9 7 5 3 1

Preface

This book is respectfully dedicated to those friends who have assisted its composition by their encouragement, criticism and suggestions: and in particular to Mr. T. E. Faber, Miss Alison Tandy, Miss Susan Wolcott, Miss Susanna Morley, and the Man in White Spats.

O. P.

Contents

The Naming of Cats

The Naming of Cats is a difficult matter,
　　It isn't just one of your holiday games;
You may think at first I'm as mad as a hatter
　　When I tell you, a cat must have THREE

　　DIFFERENT NAMES.

First of all, there's the name that the family use daily,
   Such as Peter, Augustus, Alonzo or James,
Such as Victor or Jonathan, George or Bill Bailey—
   All of them sensible everyday names.
There are fancier names if you think they sound sweeter,
   Some for the gentlemen, some for the dames:
Such as Plato, Admetus, Electra, Demeter—
   But all of them sensible everyday names.

But I tell you, a cat needs a name that's particular,

    A name that's peculiar, and more dignified,

Else how can he keep up his tail perpendicular,

    Or spread out his whiskers, or cherish his pride?

Of names of this kind, I can give you a quorum,

    Such as Munkustrap, Quaxo, or Coricopat,

Such as Bombalurina, or else Jellylorum—

    Names that never belong to more than one cat.

But above and beyond there's still one name left over,
    And that is the name that you never will guess;
The name that no human research can discover—
    But THE CAT HIMSELF KNOWS, and will never confess.

When you notice a cat in profound meditation,

    The reason, I tell you, is always the same:

His mind is engaged in a rapt contemplation

    Of the thought, of the thought, of the thought of

        his name:

        His ineffable effable

        Effanineffable

Deep and inscrutable singular Name.

The Old Gumbie Cat

I have a Gumbie Cat in mind, her name is
    Jennyanydots;
Her coat is of the tabby kind, with tiger stripes and
    leopard spots.
All day she sits upon the stair or on the steps or
    on the mat:
She sits and sits and sits and sits—and that's what makes
    a Gumbie Cat!

But when the day's hustle and bustle is done,

Then the Gumbie Cat's work is but hardly begun.

And when all the family's in bed and asleep,

She slips down the stairs to the basement to creep.

She is deeply concerned with the ways of the mice—

Their behaviour's not good and their

    manners not nice;

So when she has got them lined up on the matting,

She teaches them music, crocheting and tatting.

I have a Gumbie Cat in mind, her name is Jennyanydots;
Her equal would be hard to find, she likes the warm and
    sunny spots.
All day she sits beside the hearth or in the sun or on
    my hat:
She sits and sits and sits and sits—and that's what makes
    a Gumbie Cat!

The Old Gumbie Cat

But when the day's hustle and bustle is done,

Then the Gumbie Cat's work is but hardly begun.

As she finds that the mice will not ever keep quiet,

She is sure it is due to irregular diet

And believing that nothing is done without trying,

She sets straight to work with her baking and frying.

She makes them a mouse-cake of bread and dried peas,

And a *beautiful* fry of lean bacon and cheese.

I have a Gumbie Cat in mind, her name is Jennyanydots;
The curtain-cord she likes to wind, and tie it into
    sailor-knots.
She sits upon the window-sill, or anything that's smooth
    and flat:
She sits and sits and sits and sits—and that's what makes
    a Gumbie Cat!

The Old Gumbie Cat

But when the day's hustle and bustle is done,
Then the Gumbie Cat's work is but hardly begun.
She thinks that the cockroaches just need
    employment
To prevent them from idle and wanton destroyment.
So she's formed, from that lot of disorderly louts,
A troop of well-disciplined helpful boy-scouts,
With a purpose in life and a good deed to do—
And she's even created a Beetles' Tattoo.

So for Old Gumbie Cats let us now give three cheers—
On whom well-ordered households depend, it appears.

Growltiger's Last Stand

Growltiger was a Bravo Cat, who travelled on a barge:
In fact he was the roughest cat that ever roamed at large.
From Gravesend up to Oxford he pursued his evil aims,
Rejoicing in his title of 'The Terror of the Thames'.

Growltiger's Last Stand

His manners and appearance did not calculate to please;
His coat was torn and seedy, he was baggy at the knees;
One ear was somewhat missing, no need to tell you why,
And he scowled upon a hostile world from one
     forbidding eye.

The cottagers of Rotherhithe knew something of his fame;
At Hammersmith and Putney people shuddered at his name.
They would fortify the hen-house, lock up the silly goose,
When the rumour ran along the shore: GROWLTIGER'S
     ON THE LOOSE!

Woe to the weak canary, that fluttered from its cage;
Woe to the pampered Pekinese, that faced

   Growltiger's rage;
Woe to the bristly Bandicoot, that lurks on foreign ships,
And woe to any Cat with whom Growltiger came

   to grips!

But most to Cats of foreign race his hatred had

   been vowed;
To Cats of foreign name and race no quarter was allowed.
The Persian and the Siamese regarded him with fear—
Because it was a Siamese had mauled his missing ear.

Growltiger's Last Stand

Now on a peaceful summer night, all nature seemed at play,
The tender moon was shining bright, the barge at
    Molesey lay.
All in the balmy moonlight it lay rocking on the tide—
And Growltiger was disposed to show his
    sentimental side.

His bucko mate, GRUMBUSKIN, long since had
    disappeared,
For to the Bell at Hampton he had gone to wet his beard;
And his bosun, TUMBLEBRUTUS, he too had stol'n away—
In the yard behind the Lion he was prowling for his prey.

In the forepeak of the vessel Growltiger sate alone,
Concentrating his attention on the Lady GRIDDLEBONE.
And his raffish crew were sleeping in their barrels and
their bunks—
As the Siamese came creeping in their sampans and
their junks.

Growltiger had no eye or ear for aught but Griddlebone,
And the Lady seemed enraptured by his manly baritone,
Disposed to relaxation, and awaiting no surprise—
But the moonlight shone reflected from a hundred
bright blue eyes.

And closer still and closer the sampans circled round,

And yet from all the enemy there was not heard a sound.

The lovers sang their last duet, in danger of their lives—

For the foe was armed with toasting forks and cruel

carving knives.

Then GILBERT gave the signal to his fierce
    Mongolian horde;
With a frightful burst of fireworks the Chinese
    swarmed aboard.
Abandoning their sampans, and their pullaways and junks,
They battened down the hatches on the crew
    within their bunks.

Then Griddlebone she gave a screech, for she was
    badly skeered;
I am sorry to admit it, but she quickly disappeared.
She probably escaped with ease, I'm sure she was
    not drowned—
But a serried ring of flashing steel Growltiger did
    surround.

GROWLTIGER'S LAST STAND

The ruthless foe pressed forward, in stubborn
rank on rank;
Growltiger to his vast surprise was forced to walk the plank.
He who a hundred victims had driven to that drop,
At the end of all his crimes was forced to go ker-flip,
ker-flop.

Oh there was joy in Wapping when the news flew
through the land;
At Maidenhead and Henley there was dancing
on the strand.
Rats were roasted whole at Brentford, and at
Victoria Dock,
And a day of celebration was commanded in Bangkok.

The Rum Tum Tugger

The Rum Tum Tugger is a Curious Cat:
If you offer him pheasant he would rather have grouse.
If you put him in a house he would much prefer a flat,
If you put him in a flat then he'd rather have a house.
If you set him on a mouse then he only wants a rat,
If you set him on a rat then he'd rather chase a mouse.

Yes the Rum Tum Tugger is a Curious Cat—
    And there isn't any call for me to shout it:
        For he will do
        As he do do
            And there's no doing anything about it!

The Rum Tum Tugger is a terrible bore:
When you let him in, then he wants to be out;
He's always on the wrong side of every door,
And as soon as he's at home, then he'd like to get about.
He likes to lie in the bureau drawer,
But he makes such a fuss if he can't get out.

The Rum Tum Tugger

Yes the Rum Tum Tugger is a Curious Cat—
    And it isn't any use for you to doubt it:
      For he will do
      As he do do
        And there's no doing anything about it!

The Rum Tum Tugger is a curious beast:
His disobliging ways are a matter of habit.
If you offer him fish then he always wants a feast;
When there isn't any fish then he won't eat rabbit.
If you offer him cream then he sniffs and sneers,
For he only likes what he finds for himself;

The Rum Tum Tugger

So you'll catch him in it right up to the ears,
If you put it away on the larder shelf.

The Rum Tum Tugger is artful and knowing,
The Rum Tum Tugger doesn't care for a cuddle;
But he'll leap on your lap in the middle of your sewing,
For there's nothing he enjoys like a horrible muddle.

Yes the Rum Tum Tugger is a Curious Cat—
  And there isn't any need for me to spout it:
    For he will do
    As he do do
      And there's no doing anything about it!

The Song of the Jellicles

Jellicle Cats come out to-night
Jellicle Cats come one come all:
The Jellicle Moon is shining bright—
Jellicles come to the Jellicle Ball.

Jellicle Cats are black and white,
Jellicle Cats are rather small;
Jellicle Cats are merry and bright,
And pleasant to hear when they caterwaul.
Jellicle Cats have cheerful faces,
Jellicle Cats have bright black eyes;
They like to practise their airs and graces
And wait for the Jellicle Moon to rise.

Jellicle Cats develop slowly,

Jellicle Cats are not too big;

Jellicle Cats are roly-poly,

They know how to dance a gavotte and a jig.

Until the Jellicle Moon appears

They make their toilette and take their repose:

Jellicles wash behind their ears,

Jellicles dry between their toes.

The Song of the Jellicles

Jellicle Cats are white and black,
Jellicle Cats are of moderate size;
Jellicles jump like a jumping-jack,
Jellicle Cats have moonlit eyes.
They're quiet enough in the morning hours,
They're quiet enough in the afternoon,
Reserving their terpsichorean powers
To dance by the light of the Jellicle Moon.

Jellicle Cats are black and white,

Jellicle Cats (as I said) are small;

If it happens to be a stormy night

They will practise a caper or two in the hall.

If it happens the sun is shining bright

You would say they had nothing to do at all:

They are resting and saving themselves to be right

For the Jellicle Moon and the Jellicle Ball.

Mungojerrie and Rumpelteazer

Mungojerrie and Rumpelteazer were a very notorious
    couple of cats.
As knockabout clowns, quick-change comedians,
    tight-rope walkers and acrobats

Mungojerrie and Rumpelteazer

They had an extensive reputation. They made their
    home in Victoria Grove—
That was merely their centre of operation, for they were
    incurably given to rove.
They were very well known in Cornwall Gardens, in
    Launceston Place and in Kensington Square—
They had really a little more reputation than a couple of
    cats can very well bear.

If the area window was found ajar

And the basement looked like a field of war,

If a tile or two came loose on the roof,

Which presently ceased to be waterproof,

If the drawers were pulled out from the bedroom
chests,

And you couldn't find one of your winter vests,

Or after supper one of the girls

Suddenly missed her Woolworth pearls:

Then the family would say: 'It's that horrible cat!

It was Mungojerrie—or Rumpelteazer!'—And most of
the time they left it at that.

MUNGOJERRIE AND RUMPELTEAZER

Mungojerrie and Rumpelteazer had a very unusual gift
of the gab.

They were highly efficient cat-burglars as well, and
remarkably smart at a smash-and-grab.

They made their home in Victoria Grove. They had no
regular occupation.

They were plausible fellows, and liked to engage a
friendly policeman in conversation.

When the family assembled for Sunday dinner,
With their minds made up that they wouldn't get
thinner
On Argentine joint, potatoes and greens,
And the cook would appear from behind the scenes
And say in a voice that was broken with sorrow:
'I'm afraid you must wait and have dinner *tomorrow*!
For the joint has gone from the oven—like that!'
Then the family would say: 'It's that horrible cat!
It was Mungojerrie—or Rumpelteazer!'—And most of
the time they left it at that.

MUNGOJERRIE AND RUMPELTEAZER

Mungojerrie and Rumpelteazer had a wonderful way of
    working together.
And some of the time you would say it was luck, and
    some of the time you would say it was weather.
They would go through the house like a hurricane, and
    no sober person could take his oath
Was it Mungojerrie—or Rumpelteazer? or could you
    have sworn that it mightn't be both?

And when you heard a dining-room smash

Or up from the pantry there came a loud crash

Or down from the library came a loud *ping*

From a vase which was commonly said to be

    Ming—

Then the family would say: 'Now which was which cat?

It was Mungojerrie! AND Rumpelteazer!'—And there's

    nothing at all to be done about that!

Old Deuteronomy

Old Deuteronomy's lived a long time;

    He's a Cat who has lived many lives in succession.

He was famous in proverb and famous in rhyme

    A long while before Queen Victoria's accession.

Old Deuteronomy's buried nine wives

    And more—I am tempted to say, ninety-nine;
And his numerous progeny prospers and thrives

    And the village is proud of him in his decline.
At the sight of that placid and bland physiognomy,

    When he sits in the sun on the vicarage wall,
The Oldest Inhabitant croaks: 'Well, of all . . .

    Things . . . Can it be . . . really! . . . No! . . . Yes! . . .

        Ho! hi!

    Oh, my eye!
My sight may be failing, but yet I confess
I *believe* it is Old Deuteronomy!'

OLD DEUTERONOMY

Old Deuteronomy sits in the street,

    He sits in the High Street on market day;

The bullocks may bellow, the sheep they may bleat,

    But the dogs and the herdsmen will turn them away.

The cars and the lorries run over the kerb,

    And the villagers put up a notice: ROAD CLOSED—

So that nothing untoward may chance to disturb

    Deuteronomy's rest when he feels so disposed

Or when he's engaged in domestic economy:

    And the Oldest Inhabitant croaks: 'Well, of all . . .

    Things . . . Can it be . . . really! . . . No! . . . Yes! . . .

        Ho! hi!

        Oh, my eye!

OLD DEUTERONOMY

I'm deaf of an ear now, but yet I can guess
That the cause of the trouble is Old Deuteronomy!'

Old Deuteronomy lies on the floor
    Of the Fox and French Horn for his afternoon sleep;
And when the men say: 'There's just time for one more,'
    Then the landlady from her back parlour will peep
And say: 'Now then, out you go, by the back door,
    For Old Deuteronomy mustn't be woken—
I'll have the police if there's any uproar'—
    And out they all shuffle, without a word spoken.

Old Deuteronomy

The digestive repose of that feline's gastronomy

    Must never be broken, whatever befall:

And the Oldest Inhabitant croaks: 'Well, of all . . .

    Things . . . Can it be . . . really! . . . Yes! . . . No! . .

      Ho! hi!

      Oh, my eye!

My legs may be tottery, I must go slow

And be careful of Old Deuteronomy!'

Of the Awefull Battle of the Pekes and the Pollicles

TOGETHER WITH SOME ACCOUNT

OF THE PARTICIPATION

OF THE PUGS AND THE POMS, AND THE

INTERVENTION OF THE GREAT RUMPUSCAT

The Pekes and the Pollicles, everyone knows,

Are proud and implacable passionate foes;

It is always the same, wherever one goes.

And the Pugs and the Poms, although most people say

That they do not like fighting, will often display

Every symptom of wanting to join in the fray.

And they

    Bark bark bark bark

    Bark bark BARK BARK

Until you can hear them all over the Park.

Now on the occasion of which I shall speak
Almost nothing had happened for nearly a week
(And that's a long time for a Pol or a Peke).
The big Police Dog was away from his beat—
I don't know the reason, but most people think
He'd slipped into the Bricklayer's Arms for a drink—

Of the Awefull Battle of the Pekes and the Pollicles

And no one at all was about on the street

When a Peke and a Pollicle happened to meet.

They did not advance, or exactly retreat,

But they glared at each other, and scraped their hind feet,

And started to

> Bark bark bark bark
>
> Bark bark BARK BARK

Until you can hear them all over the Park.

Now the Peke, although people may say what they please,

Is no British Dog, but a Heathen Chinese.

And so all the Pekes, when they heard the uproar,

Some came to the window, some came to the door;

There were surely a dozen, more likely a score.

And together they started to grumble and wheeze

In their huffery-snuffery Heathen Chinese.

But a terrible din is what Pollicles like,

For your Pollicle Dog is a dour Yorkshire tyke,

And his braw Scottish cousins are snappers and biters,

And every dog-jack of them notable fighters;

And so they stepped out, with their pipers in order,

Playing *When the Blue Bonnets Came Over the Border.*

Then the Pugs and the Poms held no longer aloof,

But some from the balcony, some from the roof,

Joined in

To the din

With a

> Bark bark bark bark
>
> Bark bark BARK BARK

Until you can hear them all over the Park.

Now when these bold heroes together assembled,
The traffic all stopped, and the Underground trembled,
And some of the neighbours were so much afraid
That they started to ring up the Fire Brigade.
When suddenly, up from a small basement flat,
Why who should stalk out but the GREAT RUMPUSCAT.

His eyes were like fireballs fearfully blazing,
He gave a great yawn, and his jaws were amazing;
And when he looked out through the bars of the area,
You never saw anything fiercer or hairier.

And what with the glare of his eyes and his yawning,

The Pekes and the Pollicles quickly took warning.

He looked at the sky and he gave a great leap—

And they every last one of them scattered like sheep.

And when the Police Dog returned to his beat,

There wasn't a single one left in the street.

Mr. Mistoffelees

You ought to know Mr. Mistoffelees!
The Original Conjuring Cat—
(There can be no doubt about that).
Please listen to me and don't scoff. All his
Inventions are off his own bat.

Mr. Mistoffelees

There's no such Cat in the metropolis;
He holds all the patent monopolies
For performing surprising illusions
And creating eccentric confusions.
    At prestidigitation
        And at legerdemain
    He'll defy examination
        And deceive you again.

The greatest magicians have something to learn

From Mr. Mistoffelees' Conjuring Turn.

Presto!

 Away we go!

  And we all say: OH!

   Well I never!

   Was there ever

   A Cat so clever

    As Magical Mr. Mistoffelees!

Mr. Mistoffelees

He is quiet and small, he is black
From his ears to the tip of his tail;
He can creep through the tiniest crack,
He can walk on the narrowest rail.

He can pick any card from a pack,
He is equally cunning with dice;
He is always deceiving you into believing
That he's only hunting for mice.
   He can play any trick with a cork
      Or a spoon and a bit of fish-paste;
   If you look for a knife or a fork
      And you think it is merely misplaced—

Mr. Mistoffelees

You have seen it one moment, and then it is *gawn*!
But you'll find it next week lying out on the lawn.
   And we all say: OH!
      Well I never!
      Was there ever
      A Cat so clever
         As Magical Mr. Mistoffelees!

His manner is vague and aloof,
You would think there was nobody shyer—
But his voice has been heard on the roof
When he was curled up by the fire.
And he's sometimes been heard by the fire
When he was about on the roof—
(At least we all *heard* somebody who purred)
Which is incontestable proof

  Of his singular magical powers:
    And I have known the family to call
    Him in from the garden for hours,
      While he was asleep in the hall.

And not long ago this phenomenal Cat

Produced *seven kittens* right out of a hat!

And we all said: OH!

  Well I never!

  Did you ever

  Know a Cat so clever

   As Magical Mr. Mistoffelees!

Macavity: The Mystery Cat

Macavity's a Mystery Cat: he's called the Hidden Paw—

For he's the master criminal who can defy the Law.

He's the bafflement of Scotland Yard, the Flying Squad's
  despair:

For when they reach the scene of crime—

  Macavity's not there!

MACAVITY: THE MYSTERY CAT

Macavity, Macavity, there's no one like Macavity,
He's broken every human law, he breaks the law of
    gravity.
His powers of levitation would make a fakir stare,
And when you reach the scene of crime—
    Macavity's not there!
You may seek him in the basement, you may look up in
    the air—
But I tell you once and once again, *Macavity's not there!*

Macavity's a ginger cat, he's very tall and thin;
You would know him if you saw him, for his eyes
     are sunken in.
His brow is deeply lined with thought, his head is
     highly domed;
His coat is dusty from neglect, his whiskers are
     uncombed.
He sways his head from side to side, with movements
     like a snake;
And when you think he's half asleep, he's always
     wide awake.

MACAVITY: THE MYSTERY CAT

Macavity, Macavity, there's no one like Macavity,
For he's a fiend in feline shape, a monster of depravity.
You may meet him in a by-street, you may see him
     in the square—
But when a crime's discovered, then *Macavity's not there*!

He's outwardly respectable. (They say he cheats
  at cards.)
And his footprints are not found in any file of
  Scotland Yard's.
And when the larder's looted, or the jewel-case is rifled,
Or when the milk is missing, or another Peke's
  been stifled,
Or the greenhouse glass is broken, and the trellis
  past repair—
Ay, there's the wonder of the thing! *Macavity's not there!*

MACAVITY: THE MYSTERY CAT

And when the Foreign Office find a Treaty's gone astray,
Or the Admiralty lose some plans and drawings
    by the way,
There may be a scrap of paper in the hall or
    on the stair—
But it's useless to investigate—*Macavity's not there!*

And when the loss has been disclosed,

    the Secret Service say:

'It *must* have been Macavity!'—but he's a mile away.

You'll be sure to find him resting, or a-licking

    of his thumbs,

Or engaged in doing complicated long division sums.

Macavity: The Mystery Cat

Macavity, Macavity, there's no one like Macavity,

There never was a Cat of such deceitfulness and suavity.

He always has an alibi, and one or two to spare:

At whatever time the deed took place—

    MACAVITY WASN'T THERE!

Macavity: The Mystery Cat

And they say that all the Cats whose wicked deeds
    are widely known
(I might mention Mungojerrie, I might mention
    Griddlebone)
Are nothing more than agents for the Cat who
    all the time
Just controls their operations: the Napoleon of Crime!

Gus: The Theatre Cat

Gus is the Cat at the Theatre Door.

His name, as I ought to have told you before,

Is really Asparagus. That's such a fuss

To pronounce, that we usually call him just Gus.

GUS: THE THEATRE CAT

His coat's very shabby, he's thin as a rake,
And he suffers from palsy that makes his paw shake.
Yet he was, in his youth, quite the smartest of Cats—
But no longer a terror to mice and to rats.
For he isn't the Cat that he was in his prime;
Though his name was quite famous, he says, in its time.

And whenever he joins his friends at their club
(Which takes place at the back of the neighbouring pub)
He loves to regale them, if someone else pays,
With anecdotes drawn from his palmiest days.
For he once was a Star of the highest degree—
He has acted with Irving, he's acted with Tree.
And he likes to relate his success on the Halls,
Where the Gallery once gave him seven cat-calls.
But his grandest creation, as he loves to tell,
Was Firefrorefiddle, the Fiend of the Fell.

'I have played,' so he says, 'every possible part,
And I used to know seventy speeches by heart.
I'd extemporize back-chat, I knew how to gag,
And I knew how to let the cat out of the bag.
I knew how to act with my back and my tail;
With an hour of rehearsal, I never could fail.
I'd a voice that would soften the hardest of hearts,
Whether I took the lead, or in character parts.
I have sat by the bedside of poor Little Nell;
When the Curfew was rung, then I swung on the bell.
In the Pantomime season I never fell flat,
And I once understudied Dick Whittington's Cat.

But my grandest creation, as history will tell,

Was Firefrorefiddle, the Fiend of the Fell.'

Then, if someone will give him a toothful of gin,

He will tell how he once played a part in *East Lynne*.

At a Shakespeare performance he once walked on pat,

When some actor suggested the need for a cat.

He once played a Tiger—could do it again—

Which an Indian Colonel pursued down a drain.

And he thinks that he still can, much better than most,

Produce blood-curdling noises to bring on the Ghost.

And he once crossed the stage on a telegraph wire,

To rescue a child when a house was on fire.

Gus: The Theatre Cat

And he says: 'Now, these kittens, they do not get trained
As we did in the days when Victoria reigned.
They never get drilled in a regular troupe,
And they think they are smart, just to jump

    through a hoop.'
And he'll say, as he scratches himself with his claws,
'Well, the Theatre's certainly not what it was.
These modern productions are all very well,
But there's nothing to equal, from what I hear tell,

    That moment of mystery

    When I made history
As Firefrorefiddle, the Fiend of the Fell.'

Bustopher Jones:
The Cat About Town

Bustopher Jones is *not* skin and bones—

In fact, he's remarkably fat.

He doesn't haunt pubs—he has eight or nine clubs,

For he's the St. James's Street Cat!

He's the Cat we all greet as he walks down the street

In his coat of fastidious black:

No commonplace mousers have such well-cut trousers

Or such an impeccable back.

In the whole of St. James's the smartest of names is

The name of this Brummell of Cats;

And we're all of us proud to be nodded or bowed to

By Bustopher Jones in white spats!

His visits are occasional to the *Senior Educational*
And it is against the rules
For any one Cat to belong both to that
And the *Joint Superior Schools.*
For a similar reason, when game is in season
He is found, not at *Fox's*, but *Blimp's*;
But he's frequently seen at the gay *Stage and Screen*
Which is famous for winkles and shrimps.
In the season of venison he gives his ben'son
To the *Pothunter's* succulent bones;

And just before noon's not a moment too soon
To drop in for a drink at the *Drones*.
When he's seen in a hurry there's probably curry
At the *Siamese*—or at the *Glutton*;
If he looks full of gloom then he's lunched at the *Tomb*
On cabbage, rice pudding and mutton.

So, much in this way, passes Bustopher's day—
At one club or another he's found.
It can cause no surprise that under our eyes
He has grown unmistakably round.
He's a twenty-five pounder, or I am a bounder,
And he's putting on weight every day:

But he's so well preserved because he's observed
All his life a routine, so he'll say.
And (to put it in rhyme) 'I shall last out my time'
Is the word for this stoutest of Cats.
It must and it shall be Spring in Pall Mall
While Bustopher Jones wears white spats!

Skimbleshanks:
The Railway Cat

There's a whisper down the line at 11.39

When the Night Mail's ready to depart,

Saying 'Skimble where is Skimble has he gone

  to hunt the thimble?

We must find him or the train can't start.'

SKIMBLESHANKS: THE RAILWAY CAT

All the guards and all the porters and the
     stationmaster's daughters
They are searching high and low,
Saying 'Skimble where is Skimble for unless he's
     very nimble
Then the Night Mail just can't go.'

At 11.42 then the signal's nearly due

And the passengers are frantic to a man—

Then Skimble will appear and he'll saunter to the rear:

He's been busy in the luggage van!

    He gives one flash of his glass-green eyes

        And the signal goes 'All Clear!'

    And we're off at last for the northern part

        Of the Northern Hemisphere!

You may say that by and large it is Skimble

who's in charge

Of the Sleeping Car Express.

From the driver and the guards to the bagmen

playing cards

He will supervise them all, more or less.

Down the corridor he paces and examines all the faces

Of the travellers in the First and in the Third;

He establishes control by a regular patrol

And he'd know at once if anything occurred.

He will watch you without winking and he sees

what you are thinking

SKIMBLESHANKS: THE RAILWAY CAT

And it's certain that he doesn't approve
Of hilarity and riot, so the folk are very quiet
When Skimble is about and on the move.
    You can play no pranks with Skimbleshanks!
        He's a Cat that cannot be ignored;
    So nothing goes wrong on the Northern Mail
        When Skimbleshanks is aboard.

Oh it's very pleasant when you have found your little den

With your name written up on the door.

And the berth is very neat with a newly folded sheet

And there's not a speck of dust on the floor.

There is every sort of light—you can make it dark

    or bright;

There's a button that you turn to make a breeze.

There's a funny little basin you're supposed to wash

    your face in

And a crank to shut the window if you sneeze.

Then the guard looks in politely and will ask you
> very brightly
'Do you like your morning tea weak or strong?'
But Skimble's just behind him and was ready to
> remind him,
For Skimble won't let anything go wrong.
> And when you creep into your cosy berth
> And pull up the counterpane,
> You are bound to admit that it's very nice
> To know that you won't be bothered by mice—
> You can leave all that to the Railway Cat,
> > The Cat of the Railway Train!

In the middle of the night he is always fresh and bright;

Every now and then he has a cup of tea

With perhaps a drop of Scotch while he's keeping on

    the watch,

Only stopping here and there to catch a flea.

You were fast asleep at Crewe and so you never knew

That he was walking up and down the station;

You were sleeping all the while he was busy at Carlisle,

Where he greets the stationmaster with elation.

SKIMBLESHANKS: THE RAILWAY CAT

But you saw him at Dumfries, where he summons
the police
If there's anything they ought to know about:
When you get to Gallowgate there you do not have
to wait—
For Skimbleshanks will help you to get out!
He gives you a wave of his long brown tail
Which says: 'I'll see you again!
You'll meet without fail on the Midnight Mail
The Cat of the Railway Train.

The Ad-Dressing of Cats

You've read of several kinds of Cat,
And my opinion now is that
You should need no interpreter
To understand their character.

THE AD-DRESSING OF CATS

You now have learned enough to see
That Cats are much like you and me
And other people whom we find
Possessed of various types of mind.
For some are sane and some are mad
And some are good and some are bad
And some are better, some are worse—
But all may be described in verse.
You've seen them both at work and games,
And learnt about their proper names,
Their habits and their habitat:
But

How would you ad-dress a Cat?

So first, your memory I'll jog,
And say: A CAT IS NOT A DOG.

Now Dogs pretend they like to fight;
They often bark, more seldom bite;
But yet a Dog is, on the whole,
What you would call a simple soul.
Of course I'm not including Pekes,
And such fantastic canine freaks.
The usual Dog about the Town
Is much inclined to play the clown,
And far from showing too much pride
Is frequently undignified.

THE AD-DRESSING OF CATS

He's very easily taken in—
Just chuck him underneath the chin
Or slap his back or shake his paw,
And he will gambol and guffaw.
He's such an easy-going lout,
He'll answer any hail or shout.

Again I must remind you that
A Dog's a Dog—A CAT'S A CAT.

With Cats, some say, one rule is true:
Don't speak till you are spoken to.
Myself, I do not hold with that—
I say, you should ad-dress a Cat.
But always keep in mind that he
Resents familiarity.
I bow, and taking off my hat,
Ad-dress him in this form: O CAT!
But if he is the Cat next door,
Whom I have often met before
(He comes to see me in my flat)
I greet him with an OOPSA CAT!

The Ad-Dressing of Cats

I've heard them call him James Buz-James—
But we've not got so far as names.
Before a Cat will condescend
To treat you as a trusted friend,
Some little token of esteem
Is needed, like a dish of cream;
And you might now and then supply
Some caviare, or Strassburg Pie,
Some potted grouse, or salmon paste—
He's sure to have his personal taste.

The Ad-Dressing of Cats

(I know a Cat, who makes a habit
Of eating nothing else but rabbit,
And when he's finished, licks his paws
So's not to waste the onion sauce.)
A Cat's entitled to expect
These evidences of respect.
And so in time you reach your aim,
And finally call him by his NAME.

So this is this, and that is that:
And there's how you AD-DRESS A CAT.

Rhapsody on a Windy Night

Twelve o'clock.

Along the reaches of the street

Held in a lunar synthesis,

Whispering lunar incantations

Dissolve the floors of memory

And all its clear relations,

RHAPSODY ON A WINDY NIGHT

Its divisions and precisions,
Every street lamp that I pass
Beats like a fatalistic drum,
And through the spaces of the dark
Midnight shakes the memory
As a madman shakes a dead geranium.

Half-past one,
The street lamp sputtered,
The street lamp muttered,
The street lamp said, 'Regard that woman
Who hesitates towards you in the light of the door
Which opens on her like a grin.

You see the border of her dress
Is torn and stained with sand,
And you see the corner of her eye
Twists like a crooked pin.'

The memory throws up high and dry
A crowd of twisted things;
A twisted branch upon the beach
Eaten smooth, and polished
As if the world gave up
The secret of its skeleton,
Stiff and white.
A broken spring in a factory yard,

Rhapsody on a Windy Night

Rust that clings to the form that the strength has left
Hard and curled and ready to snap.

Half-past two,
The street lamp said,
'Remark the cat which flattens itself in the gutter,
Slips out its tongue
And devours a morsel of rancid butter.'
So the hand of a child, automatic,
Slipped out and pocketed a toy that was running along
the quay.
I could see nothing behind that child's eye.
I have seen eyes in the street

Trying to peer through lighted shutters,
And a crab one afternoon in a pool,
An old crab with barnacles on his back,
Gripped the end of a stick which I held him.

Half-past three,
The lamp sputtered,
The lamp muttered in the dark.

The lamp hummed:
'Regard the moon,
La lune ne garde aucune rancune,
She winks a feeble eye,

RHAPSODY ON A WINDY NIGHT

She smiles into corners.
She smoothes the hair of the grass.
The moon has lost her memory.
A washed-out smallpox cracks her face,
Her hand twists a paper rose,
That smells of dust and old Cologne,
She is alone
With all the old nocturnal smells
That cross and cross across her brain.'
The reminiscence comes
Of sunless dry geraniums
And dust in crevices,
Smells of chestnuts in the streets,

And female smells in shuttered rooms,

And cigarettes in corridors

And cocktail smells in bars.

The lamp said,

'Four o'clock,

Here is the number on the door.

Memory!

You have the key,

The little lamp spreads a ring on the stair,

Mount.

The bed is open; the tooth-brush hangs on the wall,

Put your shoes at the door, sleep, prepare for life.'

The last twist of the knife.